The Littlest Tree

By Charles Tazewell

Illustrated by Karen A. Jerome

Ideals Children's Books • Nashville, Tennessee
an imprint of Hambleton-Hill Publishing, Inc.

To Laura and Michael, for all your hugs and kisses.
  —Auntie Jerome

Text copyright © 1997 by Charles Tazewell
Illustrations copyright © 1997 by Hambleton-Hill Publishing, Inc.

Published by Ideals Children's Books
An imprint of Hambleton-Hill Publishing, Inc.
Nashville, Tennessee 37218

Printed and bound in Mexico

Library of Congress Cataloging-in-Publication Data
Tazewell, Charles.
    The littlest tree / by Charles Tazewell ; illustrated by Karen A.
Jerome. — 1st ed.
        p.   cm.
    Summary: Solomon and everyone else in the Celestial City are
surprised when a paltry sprig, which has been lovingly decorated by a
group of orphans in a war-torn city, is chosen to be the Son's
Birthday Tree.
    ISBN 1-57102-121-3 (hardcover)
    [1. Christmas trees—Fiction. 2. Christmas—Fiction. 3. Heaven—
Fiction.] I. Jerome, Karen A., ill. II. Title.
PZ7.T219Lt   1997
[E]—dc21   97-5873
                                                                CIP
                                                                 AC

The illustrations in this book were rendered in watercolor and colored pencil.
The text type is set in Goudy.
The display type is set in Caslon Open and Goudy BoldItalic.

10 9 8 7 6 5 4 3 2

In Heaven, long ago, the Lord decreed that every tree chosen for His Son's birthday—and which was destined to wear a scrap of holiday ribbon, a tatter of tinsel, or even a child-strung grimy garland of popcorn—would remain "evergreen" and would never die. At the very instant the tree was taken from its rooted place, its replica, exact in every twig and needle, would grow in the Forest of the Nativity.

It is a vast and beautiful place, this Forest of the Nativity. A merry, heartwarming place with its millions of Christmas trees from Earth's hundreds of merry, heartwarming Christmases. Isadore, of the green robe and thumb, is at the gatehouse—and, when it is early winter by our earthly year, he is the most overworked saint in Paradise.

Working sunlight and starlight, he and his ink-bespattered scribes scrupulously record the arrival of every tree. Then, throughout all the exciting days that lead up to Christmas, the gatehouse is as filled with scratching as the busiest henhouse, as their feathered pens compile a complete history of each tree's counterpart down on Earth. No smile, no touch, no word, no blessing or honor bestowed upon a single tree must go unnoticed. Nothing, no matter how small or how seemingly insignificant, must be overlooked. On Christmas Eve, His Son will come to the Forest to choose the one most loved for His Birthday Tree—and He will point and He will ask Saint Isadore, "Did this one stand in a corner of a room or in the very center of someone's Christmas?" . . . "Did a child look up at this tree with wonder and perhaps whisper My name?"—"What man or woman loved this small evergreen? . . . And why? . . . And how much?"

The seven days that precede Christmas are almost unbearable for the cherubs—each trying to guess which tree will be the Son's choice.

"I'll bet," whispers one, "it'll be that tree!"

"No!" asserts another. "The one over there!"

"It's no use our picking one out," mourns a third cherub. "We never guess right. I guess nobody ever guesses right."

"Solomon does!" cries a fourth. "He's never missed yet! Let's go ask him which one will be the Birthday Tree!"—and off they race in search of the old gentleman.

And strange as it may seem, this Solomon rightfully deserves the reputation he has among cherubs for his infallible guesses. He is a sage—a man of much learning and who, before immigration to the Celestial City, was an earthly king highly respected for his judgment and wisdom.

Citizens of the Celestial City always tell new arrivals that on Christmas after Christmas, Solomon has predicted which tree would be the Birthday Tree—and he has always been right. That is—all except once!

On that war-torn Christmas, Solomon—and all Paradise—was arrayed in glorious confusion because his prediction was as wrong as a square halo.

The tree he chose was one of the most beautiful ever to appear in the Forest of the Nativity. A stately pyramid of greenery—so tall that it dwarfed all that year's Christmas trees. Its counterpart stood in the heart of a great city. War-weary millions had looked on it and loved it. At its feet, people had sung carols, murmured prayers, and lifted up their eyes to wish on the star that crowned it for peace on earth and good will toward all men forever and ever amen. Since every needle had been touched by love, it had to be the Birthday Tree.

But it wasn't.

All eyes were turned toward the Street of Miracles and the Heavenly Choir was singing "O Birthday Tree" when Saint Isadore carried the Son's choice into the great Plaza of Eternity.

The light of every burning star in the firmament wavered before the gasp of astonishment from the assembled multitude, and the voice of the Heavenly Choir faltered and was still.

The Birthday Tree wasn't really a tree at all. It was a paltry sprig—an insignificant sprout—a miserable splinter not worth a tenth, not a thousandth, not even a millionth of a widow's mite! It was a crooked, luckless, wretched, stunted, sap-starved, and barkbeggared piece of scrub; it was the littlest tree in the whole kingdom, born of a windwandering seed to live among weeds and keep stringy root and scrawny stem together by begging scraps of sunlight and droplets of leftover rain.

To this day, Solomon and many others still firmly believe that Saint Isadore made a grave and unforgivable mistake—and that the Son was too kind and too compassionate to correct him.

This is a lot of halo-dust and wing-breeze.

To save Solomon and those others from an eternity of wondering and doubt, here is a true account—taken from Isadore's files in the gatehouse of the Forest of the Nativity—of the Littlest Tree.

The Littlest Tree wasn't sought—nor was it come upon accidentally and hailed with cries of delight.

It wasn't cut with an ax nor was it proudly carried off to its appointed place.

It grew in a roadside ditch, noisome with the debris of war, some distance from a bomb-devastated city.

One could walk the rubble-piled streets of the city that year and never meet a reminder of Christmas. The shop windows, which had been magic glasses for children to look through and see a holiday wonderland of marvelous toys, delectable sweetmeats, and mouth-watering pastries and puddings, were long gone with the bombers. Anyone gazing through the now twisted, glassless rims could see a nightmare world where rats, ghostlike with plaster dust, prowled the tumbled masonry and fire-blackened beams.

Gone were the rotund shopkeepers who had decorated the windows with lights and ribbons and tinsel; gone were their fat, jolly wives who had called out a hearty greeting to every gift-laden customer as he or she left the shop; gone were the wide-eyed children whose cold, Christmas-nipped noses had been a festoon of red buttons across every treasure-filled window.

Oh, there were people still living in the city. The flotsam and jetsam left behind by the high tide of war. And there were children. Some of them had fathers, mothers, or other relatives to look after them. Less fortunate were the orphans, the lost, and the abandoned. The unwanted, the untended, the unloved. These ran in small fox-packs—living in the cellars of ruined buildings and filling their ever-hungry stomachs by wily begging and sly theft.

The leader of each pack was usually the oldest, the strongest, and most pugnacious member. Johann met all of these requirements. He had squeaked by his twelfth birthday; he had arm muscles as big as hickory nuts; he had a tongue that could make the most polite oath sound unprintable.

In Johann's pack were Lucas, Otto, Ernst, Hugo, Anton, and Laus. To be truthful, Laus really wasn't a bona fide member. In fact, Laus was too small, too fragile, and too young to be much of anything.

Johann found her in the cellar one day when he returned from a foray.

"What is that?" he demanded.

"What does it look like?" answered Otto. "It's a girl."

"How did she get here?"

"She followed us," said Ernst.

"We tried to chase her off but she wouldn't go," explained Anton.

"Where did she come from?"

"Who knows?" shrugged Otto. "She doesn't even know her name."

"We can't have a girl on our hands," snarled Johann. "On top of that, she's a baby—not two years out of her diapers. Hugo—Anton—take her out and lose her!"

"You're the leader! Who goes and who stays is your job," argued Hugo.

"All right—all right!" shouted Johann, seizing the child's hand. "I will get rid of her myself!"

Darkness had fallen but Johann knew the streets well. He walked for ten minutes and came upon a doorway that spilled light into the night.

"Stay here," he said, disengaging her hand from his. "Maybe somebody good will find you."

Squaring his thin shoulders, he stalked off. In a moment, he heard her footsteps following him. Not even turning his head to look, he walked faster. His ears told him that small feet were running and stumbling after him.

"Two can play at this game!" growled Johann—and he ran down the street and around a corner to hide behind a broken wall. He waited and listened but there was no sound.

Perhaps she fell, he thought. Maybe she tumbled down a cellar-hole where nobody would ever find her. Well . . . it wouldn't take a minute to look and see.

He retraced his steps. He would never have noticed the small ball rolled up in the rubble-strewn gutter if it hadn't been for its heart-stricken weeping.

"Ah, well," said Johann. "Anything so little couldn't eat much or crowd us any."

Johann carried her back to the cellar.

"I've changed my mind," he announced belligerently. "We need someone to watch things when we're out. That's her job and we'll call her 'Laus!'" He pinched her ear. "You hear that? A laus is a little bug, and you, little bug, crawled into my heart."

Somehow, life in the cellar seemed to be less dismal now that Laus' blonde head was there. The boys, on their expeditions in search of food, tried to return with some trinket that would make her blue eyes grow big and round. It didn't have to be much. A bit of mirror. A broken toy. A chipped cup. Johann, their leader, was more practical. He remembered a prewar requisite for child nutrition. A certain supply sergeant may still curse the son-of-a-magician who got away with a full case of powdered milk.

One evening in early December, they were huddled around a small flicker of fire in the cellar.

"You know something?" said Otto. "It's getting on to Christmas."

"Is it?" asked Ernst.

"Christmas—Hallowmas—Michaelmas—who cares?" growled Johann.

"My family had elegant Christmases," said Anton. "Our very last Christmas we had a turkey—honest, I'm not lying to you! A turkey dinner with all the trimmings!"

"And the Christmas presents!" sighed Otto. "Skates—and lead soldiers in red coats—and a muffler so thick and warm and fleecy that your throat thought it was summer even on the coldest day!"

"I remember the Christmas tree best," sighed Ernst. "Would you believe it— the other night, I dreamt about the last one we had. There was our house—not fallen down but just as it used to be—and in the front window, behind the lace curtains, was my mother and our Christmas tree!"

"What's a Christmas tree?" asked Laus.

"Didn't you ever see one?" said Johann.

"No." Laus shook her head. "No, I never."

"Imagine that!" laughed Hugo. "She never saw a Christmas tree!"

"What's so funny about it?" snapped Johann. "How could she remember the good Christmases—she's too young."

"But what is one?" asked Laus.

"Oh, it's nothing much," said Johann. "Just a tree with a lot of junk on it. Colored balls. Sparkly stuff. A few lights."

"And a star up on the top," added Ernst.

"Sure—any kind of silly trash. Come on, Little Bug—," he slapped her bottom, "time to drink your milk and scoot off to bed!"

The matter might have ended then and there if it hadn't been for a sickly green branch protruding from the underpart of a military vehicle that Johann saw while looking for food the next morning.

Johann squatted down and looked under the car to see if this might be some new kind of camouflage to foil enemy snipers. He studied it and shrugged his shoulders. It wasn't anything that could be eaten or traded or sold. A bush—or perhaps a little tree. Rocking on his heels, his eyes examined each twisted branch and the scraggy stem. Then, after a furtive glance over his shoulder—because no two uniforms ever seemed to agree on what was essential and what was surplus— he removed the tree from its prison and carried it off to the cellar.

In his gatehouse, a distraught Saint Isadore dipped his quill and wrote: "A strange sort of scrub tree has just appeared in the Forest of the Nativity. My chief scribe tells me that it was torn up by the roots and that its counterpart is now wedged between some rods under a military vehicle. Why the Proprietor considers it a Christmas tree is beyond my understanding. I shall number it 99,864 and await further information."

That night, after Laus was asleep, Johann picked up the stub of candle and beckoned imperiously to the members of his pack to follow him. He led them over the fallen stones to the adjoining cellar. Holding the candle high, he pointed dramatically to a corner.

"There, now!" he said with great pride. "Just what do you think of that?"

"What is it?" asked Hugo.

"What is it! Are you trying to prove you're an idiot? It's a tree!"

"Ho!" hooted Anton. "It's not like any tree I've ever seen!"

"It's a worthless bush," announced Otto, "and it won't burn because it's too green."

"Even dried out it wouldn't be worth the chopping," added Ernst. "What would you have? Two pieces of kindling."

"Did I even mention a fire?" demanded Johann. "Why do I waste my time on such stupid people? Now open your eyes and look at it—this is a Christmas tree!"

"That stick?" laughed Hugo.

"All right!" conceded Johann. "Perhaps it is only a stick! But tell me this—has Laus ever seen a real Christmas tree? Will she compare it with the ones that we can remember? No, she has not and will not! Besides—," he looked at the tree with half-closed eyes, "I do not think it will look at all bad when it is decorated."

"Decorated?" asked an incredulous Anton.

"Decorated with what?" muttered Otto.

"Do I have to tell you what things go on a Christmas tree? Go out and find them!" commanded Johann. "Start looking tomorrow morning!"

And they did! Red lipsticks, green ink, a bottle of blueing—and some yellow twine! A gearshift knob, a Brigadier General's silver insignia—all were brought back to place on the Littlest Tree.

The last decoration was put on two nights before Christmas. Johann, Lucas, Otto, Ernst, Hugo, and Anton all agreed that nothing more could be done to help the appearance of the Littlest Tree.

"Shall we let Laus see it now?" asked Otto.

"Why not?" shrugged Johann. "The thing's getting more brown and dried-up by the minute. I'll wake her and bring her in. Get those candle stubs lighted!" he called as he went clambering over the rubble. In the next cellar, he bent over Laus and tapped her nose with his finger.

"Wake up!" he whispered. "Wake up—we've got a surprise for you!"

"What?" she asked sleepily. "What, Johann?"

"A surprise! Something you've never seen! It's of Christmas! Come let me show you!"

With her small hand in his, he led her to where the Littlest Tree stood in its meager glory.

"Merry Christmas!" called the boys.

"What do you think of this?" asked Otto.

"It's a Christmas tree!" laughed Ernst.

"For you, Laus!" added Hugo.

"Do you like it?" beamed Lucas.

"Why doesn't she say something?" scowled Otto.

"Hey! Hey—she's crying!" said Anton.

"Nonsense!" growled Hugo. "Why should anyone cry over a Christmas tree?"

"Well, she is so crying! See those tears on her cheeks?"

"So whose business is it?" asked Johann. "Come on—let's do it up right. 'O Tannenbaum'—and I want to hear everybody singing!"

Laus crept toward the Littlest Tree—fearful that it might vanish if she approached it too hastily. Then, at its foot, she looked up. To Laus, who had seen nothing but ugliness and ruin and corruption, this miserable outcast that masqueraded as a Christmas tree had a breathtaking beauty that was beyond belief or comprehension. This was the tallest, the greenest, and the most stately tree that had ever sprung from Earth and grown toward His Heaven.

The massive trunk was set in an urn of burnished gold. Each sturdy, outstretched bough—bending low with the weight of its lush greenery—wore a jeweled garland, an intricate silver chain, a gleaming diamond pendant. On every branch, even the smallest, there was a ruby, an emerald, a turquoise, or a topaz that was as big and as round as the largest and most astounded "Oh" in a delighted "Oh, My!" Up on top, at the very topmost tip, there was a star! A shining star which caught the light of the candle and twinkled—much as His Son's eye is said to twinkle when He hears that all His people are keeping Christmas.

Laus didn't see, for such is the blindness of childhood, that the golden urn which held the measly stem was only an army helmet dabbed with stolen yellow paint; that the diamond pendants were merely shards of glass dug from the rubble; that the precious gems were purloined gearshift knobs and the silver chains were foil from the trash barrels of the military canteens; that the star came not from Bethlehem and it had never risen an inch higher than the collar of a Brigadier General.

It was an ugly, little tree dressed in rubbish—but Laus bent over and touched a crooked, misshapen branch.

"Christmas tree—," she whispered, "Oh Christmas tree, I love you! I love you more than anything—!" and she planted a moist kiss and left a single tear on its dried-up greenery.

Yes—it was the littlest tree one would ever see. Yet on Christmas Eve, its counterpart was carried away by Saint Isadore into the great Forest of the Nativity. There, it stood for all Heaven to see and know as The Birthday Tree of His Only Son.

Solomon, the wise, saw only a paltry sprig—an insignificant sprout.

But the Son saw none of these imperfections. He saw a tree that had grown to wear a child's kiss and a child's tear.

There was no doubt in His Mind when He chose the Littlest Tree as His Birthday Tree.

Tree 99,864, above all others, was the most loved tree on His Earth that Christmas.